Don't Want to Go!

For Mark

First U.S. edition 2010

Library of Congress Cataloging-in-Publication Data is available.

Library of Congress Catalog Card Number pending

ISBN 978-0-7636-5091-9

10 11 12 13 14 15 16 TWPS 10 9 8 7 6 5 4 3 2 1

Printed in Singapore

This book was typeset in Century Old Style.
The illustrations were done in gouache.

Candlewick Press
99 Dover Street
Somerville, Massachusetts 02144

visit us at www.candlewick.com

Don't Want to Go!

Shirley Hughes

CANDLEWICK PRESS

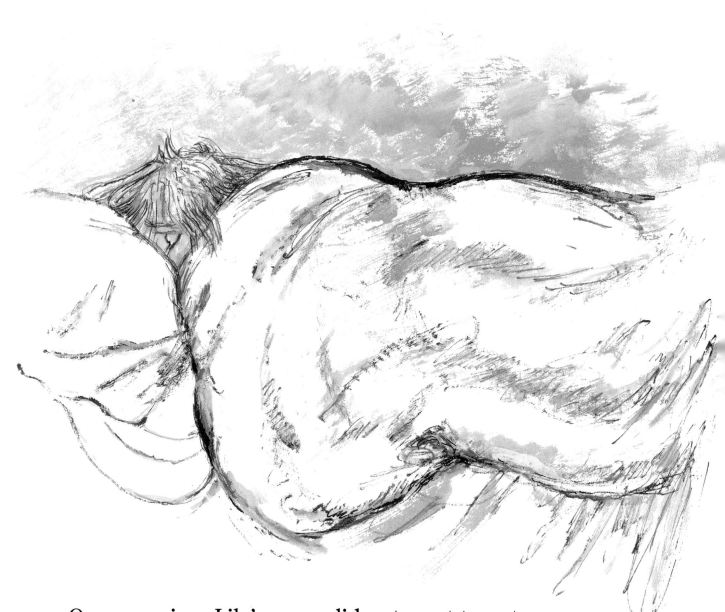

One morning, Lily's mom did not want to get up.
She just lay there with her eyes closed. She said
that her head ached and her throat was sore and
she felt hot and shivery all over.

"Mom has the flu," Dad said as he gave Lily her breakfast. "She needs to stay in bed today, and I have to go to work." He looked worried.

"Who will look after me, then?" Lily wanted to know.

Dad was already on the phone.
When he hung up he said, "Guess what!
You're going to play at Melanie's house!
You're going to play at Melanie's house!
Won't that be fun?"

"Who's Melanie?" asked Lily.

"You remember Melanie!
You've been to her house
before. She lives just near
here on Wesley Avenue.
She has a big boy
named Jack and
a baby named Sam!"

"I've dropped the
yellow bit of my egg
on the floor," was
all Lily said.

"There will be lots of nice toys to play with," Dad said. He wiped Lily's mouth and mopped the floor. Then he buttoned her into her jacket and put on her hat and mittens.

"Don't want to go!" said Lily.

"I'll take you in the stroller, it will be quicker," said Dad as he tucked Bobbo in beside her. "Off we go!" he said in a very jolly voice.

They were just turning onto Wesley Avenue when Dad discovered that Lily's mittens were gone.

"I'm sure we put them on before we left the house," he said.

He turned the stroller around. They were halfway home before they found the mittens.

Dad picked them up and put them back on Lily's hands. Then he pushed the stroller full steam ahead till they reached Melanie's front door.

It was a yellow door, the color
of the inside of Lily's egg.

"Here we are!" said Dad.

"Don't want to go!" said Lily.
She went all stiff and would
not get out of the stroller.

But just then the door opened,
and there was Melanie with a
smiling face, holding baby
Sam. He said, "Da!" and held
out his fat little hand to Lily in
a friendly way.

Lily and Dad stepped into Melanie's hall. Lily was clutching Bobbo very tightly. Dad knelt down. He took off Lily's hat and mittens and gave her a big hug. "Have a good time, darling," he said. "I'll finish work early."

"Don't want to stay," said Lily in a tiny voice.

As the door closed on Dad, Lily opened her mouth to give a big yell. But at that moment a little dog ran into the hall. He was white with brown ears and patches. He ran straight up to Lily and licked her hand.

Lily liked that. She decided not to yell after all.

"His name's Ringo," Melanie told her. "And it looks as though he likes you a lot."

They all went into the kitchen. It was warm in there.
Ringo's basket was in the corner.

Melanie put Sam in his high chair. "Sam's going to have
some toast and jam. Would you like some?" she asked.

"Don't want toast," said Lily. She forgot to say thank you.

While Sam sat in his chair and ate toast and jam, Lily and
Bobbo sat under the table.

When Sam was done, Melanie lifted him out of his high chair and put him on the floor because he was a crawling baby.

Sam wanted to play peekaboo with Lily.

And Lily couldn't help laughing
because he was so funny.

When Sam was tired, Melanie took him upstairs for a nap. Then she spread some magazine pictures across the kitchen table. She fetched some glue and a big scrapbook.

"Would you like to do some pasting?" she asked.

"No, thank you," said Lily.

"Well, perhaps you would like to help me choose, then," said Melanie.

So Lily chose where the different pictures were to go. She chose a piece of cake on a lady's head and a rabbit riding on a fish, a shiny red car in a bed, and a building balancing on a chest of drawers. When they had finished, it was a very interesting book.

"You can show it to your dad when he comes to collect you," said Melanie.

Sam was cross when he woke up. Tears
trickled down his cheeks and his mouth was
a miserable O shape, showing two tiny teeth.

But when he caught sight of Lily, he
stopped crying, little by little, and began
to hiccup instead.

"He won't do that for me!" said Melanie.
"Thank you, Lily."

At lunchtime Lily helped to spoon food into Sam's mouth. A lot went into the wrong places but Sam did not seem to mind.

Soon it was time to pick up Sam's big brother, Jack, from school.

"Don't want to—" began Lily.

But Melanie said quickly, "Ringo's coming too and you can help hold his leash if you like."

So Lily held Ringo while
Melanie fixed the leash
onto his collar.

Lily helped hold on to Ringo
all the way to Jack's school.

Sometimes he pulled on
the leash and wanted to run
ahead so badly that they could
hardly keep up with him.

And sometimes he wanted to
stop and sniff around.

They all had to run
the last bit very fast
to get there in time.

Ringo went nearly crazy with joy when Jack came running out of school. Jack had curly hair and a beautiful smile with no front teeth.

When they got back, Jack made some cardboard boxes into boats, and they pretended that Lily and Sam and Bobbo were sailing far out to sea.

Ringo stayed on the seashore and kept a lookout.

Then they sat together on the sofa and watched television—all except Sam, who played on the floor. Ringo lay between Jack and Lily with his head on Lily's lap.

While they were sitting there, the doorbell rang. When Melanie went to answer it, Lily heard Dad's voice in the hall.

"You've been having a great time, I hear," he said, putting his head around the sitting-room door. "I've come to collect you, as promised."

And he held out Lily's jacket.

But Lily snuggled deeper into the sofa
and hugged Ringo to her chest.

"Don't want to go," she said.